This book is dedicated to all of the young men in the world who have dreamed a dream that they were skeptical about and didn't think or know if they could achieve or obtain it. Those young men who dreamed the impossible and thought *IF I ONLY COULD*! With hard work and dedication, you can achieve great, great things—things that you would not have believed were possible. Don't let anyone keep you from your dreams and goals and what truly belongs to you.

To my parents, all four of them. To Valerie and Curtis Wideman, I would like to say THANK YOU for being there, teaching and guiding me, never losing sight of what was truly important, and keeping me on track, focused, and grounded. Thank you for having enough wit to pass the baton to Diane and Estes Hood, affectionately called Momma D and Poppa E, who took me the rest of the way and gave me nothing but love, encouragement, and support. I will love you always. To the love of my life, Grandma Minnie Mae, we did it and I want you to know that I will never forget all of our picnics and you being there for me my entire lifetime. Daddy Bill, what can I say, I have had so many memorable times and enjoyable laughs with you. Thank you for our Kangaroos School Sessions, I learned a lot. To the best brother in the ENTIRE world, Kyle man, I wouldn't have made it without you and you know that I love you for it. To everyone who has had a hand in helping me to succeed so far in life, I truly thank you all.

I saved the best for last, George Woolridge, affectionately called Coach G. Without you none of this would have EVER been possible. Man, you taught me and exposed me to a new world that I never knew existed. I love you man, you are a GREAT COACH and you have a GREAT gift that God has blessed you with.

Again to ALL of the young men in the world, as you can see there is so much truth in the old African proverb, "It takes a village to raise a child," just look at

www.mascotbooks.com

Top Dog

For more information, please contact:
Mascot Books
560 Herndon Parkway #120
Herndon, VA 20170
info@mascotbooks.com

Library of Congress Control Number: 2016917453

CPSIA Code: PRT1216A
ISBN-13: 978-1-63177-921-3

Printed in the United States

TOP DOG

by Curtis Wideman

illustrated by Sayantan Halder

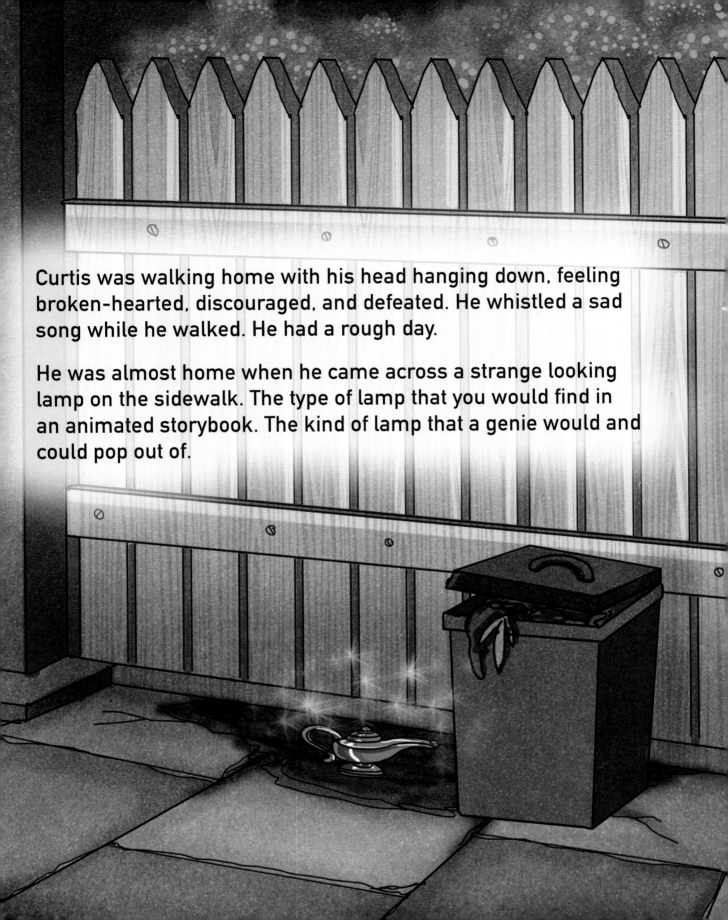

Curtis was walking home with his head hanging down, feeling broken-hearted, discouraged, and defeated. He whistled a sad song while he walked. He had a rough day.

He was almost home when he came across a strange looking lamp on the sidewalk. The type of lamp that you would find in an animated storybook. The kind of lamp that a genie would and could pop out of.

Excited and curious, Curtis picked up the lamp, rubbed it, and to his surprise, out popped the strangest looking thing that he had ever seen. A genie, a REAL LIVE GENIE! The genie was a little slow, wobbly, and rusty for, you see, he had been in the lamp for a VERY, VERY, VERY, long time.

Curtis could not believe his eyes. "Hello young man," said the genie. "My name is Coach G and who do I have the pleasure of meeting? Why do you look so sad? You summoned me, so how can I be of help to you?"

"What did you say?" Curtis was lost and confused. He wanted to run, but his feet wouldn't move.

Curtis regained his composure and said, "My name is Curtis, Curtis Wideman, and I didn't make the track team. I tried out as a sprinter, but I wasn't fast enough. Can you really help me?"

"Why, of course! If you want my help, then you shall have it, but only if you're willing to do some hard work. Are you willing to do what it takes?"

Curtis nodded his head and said, "Yes, yes I am!"

"All right then, Curtis," said Coach G. "I want you to go back to the school and try out for the track team again. This time, try out for the throwing team called the E-Town Throwers."

Curtis replied, "But, I didn't make it!"

"I think that this time you will make it, and if you do, I promise to grant you three wishes."

Curtis thought for a moment and said, "Why not, I have nothing to lose."

Curtis did as Coach G said and went back to the school and tried out again. This time he tried out for the shot put, disc, and hammer throw. This time speed was not a factor, strength was—and Curtis had the strength of two boys his age. Much to his surprise, he made the TEAM!

Curtis was so excited that he ran straight over to Coach G on the sidelines and gave him the biggest hug EVER. "THANK YOU! THANK YOU! THANK YOU!" Curtis yelled, and Coach G gave him a big, big smile.

"Now about my three wishes…" Curtis said. Coach G told Curtis to think long and hard about his wishes because he could only grant wishes for things that Curtis could not achieve himself. Curtis thought for a while then said, "For my first wish, I want to become the best and greatest athlete in the world."

Coach G shook his head and said, "Curtis, I can't grant that wish for you because you can achieve that all by yourself. You see, with hard work and dedication, you can become the best and greatest athlete in the world all by yourself. Wish denied."

Curtis frowned and thought some more. He realized that he had just wasted one of his wishes. *I must be more careful with my second wish.*

"Then for my next wish, I wish for you to be my personal track coach. Coach G, if you will be my personal coach, I promise I'll work hard. I know you can train me to be the best."

Coach G looked at Curtis and said, "Your wish has been granted. Now put these on."

Coach G made Curtis practice before and after school, and even after team practice. He had to work out extra hard in the weight room so he could grow stronger and stronger. Together, Curtis and Coach G put in a lot of hard work and dedication.

This helped Curtis to become a great thrower. Most importantly, Curtis learned all about technique, and it gave him the discipline that he needed to achieve his goals. With all of this hard work and dedication, it was finally time for Curtis to see his progress.

It was the day of the school's big track meet, and throwing was one of the main events. Athletes from every school in the area were here to compete.

Curtis took first place in every throwing event that he competed in. He broke every school record in his area. He not only made himself proud, but he made Coach G over-the-moon proud as well.

Since Curtis had done so well at the track meet, he knew it was time to ask for his final wish. "I wish for special powers so I can be an Olympic gold medal athlete!"

Coach G shook his head. "I can't grant your wish. Remember, I cannot grant any wish that you can achieve by yourself. Again, with hard work and dedication, you can become an Olympic gold medal athlete all by yourself. But you have to put in the work. Wish denied."

Curtis frowned, then smiled. "I know with your help and hard work, I can make it happen."

While Curtis was dreaming of going to the Olympics with Coach G's help and guidance, Coach G was trying to find a way to break it to Curtis that it was time for him to leave. His mission had been accomplished.

Curtis frowned, then smiled. "I know with your help and hard work, I can make it happen."

While Curtis was dreaming of going to the Olympics with Coach G's help and guidance, Coach G was trying to find a way to break it to Curtis that it was time for him to leave. His mission had been accomplished.

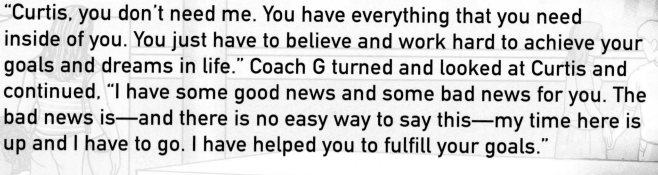

"Curtis, you don't need me. You have everything that you need inside of you. You just have to believe and work hard to achieve your goals and dreams in life." Coach G turned and looked at Curtis and continued, "I have some good news and some bad news for you. The bad news is—and there is no easy way to say this—my time here is up and I have to go. I have helped you to fulfill your goals."

Curtis was devastated, confused, and in a state of shock.

Coach G went on to say, "The good news is…well do you see that man sitting down there?" Coach G pointed to a man writing on a notepad and sitting on the bottom bleacher. Curtis nodded. "He is a college scouting and recruiting coach. He watched you compete at the meet and wants to meet you personally. He wants to give you a track scholarship. Curtis, you will be in good hands with him, and you will achieve great feats."

Even after Coach G was gone, Curtis never forgot his advice. It felt like Coach G was always nearby rooting for him.

And he was. Curtis doesn't know it, but Coach has been there every step of the way, and needless to say, Coach G still has two more wishes to grant Curtis on the road to the 2020 Olympics.

"The 2020 Olympics get closer every day, so LET'S GET TO WORK! Technique, Technique, Technique!"

"If you can dream it, you can achieve it.
Lesson well learned, Curtis!
Now give back!"

ABOUT THE AUTHOR, CURTIS WIDEMAN

Curtis Wideman was born and raised in Evanston, Illinois and graduated from Evanston Township High School (ETHS) in 2011. Curtis continued his education at Southern Illinois University in Carbondale, Illinois through a track scholarship. Curtis was a vital member of the Evanston Township High School track team from 2009 to 2011 as well as the Southern Illinois University (SIU) track team from 2011 to 2015. Curtis graduated from Southern Illinois University in May 2015 with a Bachelor of Arts in Radio, Television, and Digital Media. Curtis is currently in graduate school at SIU and will graduate in May 2017 with a Master's in Sports Studies. Curtis would like to work with at-risk youth by using sports as a vehicle to help them to continue their education. Curtis is also a member of the Alpha Phi Alpha Fraternity, Mu Kappa Lambda Chapter.

ABOUT THE GENIE, GEORGE WOOLRIDGE

George Woolridge, "Coach G," is also a native Evanstonian and an alumni of Evanston Township High School (ETHS). Coach G continued his education at Western Illinois University in Macomb, Illinois after he graduated from ETHS. Coach G was a vital part of the Western Illinois University track team; he was a thrower as well. This is where his true love for throwing began. He threw the discus 180, the shot 58, and the hammer 190. Coach G has been a track coach for Evanston Township High School for the past thirty-one years. Coach G has been very instrumental in helping other young athletes to achieve, to love track, and to achieve great feats. There should be more coaches just like him; he is truly worth his weight in GOLD!